Edwin Ross Champlin

On the White-Birch Road

Edwin Ross Champlin

On the White-Birch Road

ISBN/EAN: 9783337341848

Printed in Europe, USA, Canada, Australia, Japan

Cover: Foto ©Andreas Hilbeck / pixelio.de

More available books at **www.hansebooks.com**

ON
THE WHITE-BIRCH ROAD.

BY

EDWIN R. CHAMPLIN.

AUTHOR'S EDITION.
MAY 4, 1891.

E. A. STILLMAN, PRINTER,
WESTERLY. R. I.

Ever since my eyes have seen
The rural hosts of forest green,
And tall white birches sentinel the doors
Of cities; when all day down pours
The sun's straight heat, I haste to that green shade;
But ever, day and night, my muse hath made
Her path between white branches, slim and tall,
And loves those slender birches best of all.

On the White-Birch Road.

A SONG OF AN IMMORTAL.

[John Boyle O'Reilly, born in County Meath, Ireland, June 28th, 1844; died in Hull, Massachusetts, August 10th, 1890.]

LL is silent, moveless now
    Where, a little while ago,
    Mystic currents used to flow—
All know why, but who knows how?
    And where men could see the glow
    Of the soul that dwelt below,
Now they see no face, no brow.

All is changed since *he* has gone—
    He who made the summer day
       When his light of life went out
    Darker than the darkest way
       He had ever sung about:
And we say his life is done,
Battle fought and garland won.

But our inner sight prevails;
   To our inner hearing comes
      Something dearer than we heard—
      Music of a subtler chord
   Than the living poet thrums;
All old strains our spirit hails
   Through celestial tympanums,
And the flame of life we knew
   Burns a ceaseless, steady light,
   Leading dull eyes through the night
To the spirit's sky of blue;
Like a spark from God it burns—
   Purer, clearer, day by day,
   As the youth-mists clear away,
And our dark to daylight turns.

He whom we shall see no more
   Face to face and hand to hand,
   Though cut off from this small land,
Doth a universe explore.
In the world of Memory,
   Where our best-beloved dwell,
   And there is no sad farewell,
There is he whom none may see
In the way that was so dear;

And his gifts of love and song
 Are more beautiful and strong
Than they seemed when he was here.
He was valorous, we knew:
 He was Freedom's servitor:
 Now we know his only war
Was for Freedom; to her true.
In the darkness of the day
 He his torch of truth upbore,
 And that light is borne before
By new hands that feel its sway.
He was tender as a flower:
 We could see it in his eyes,
 In his questions and replies:
Poor men saw it in his dower.
Now that tenderness has grown:
 Deep and broad it was, a part
 Of the greatness of his heart,
That before was little known.
So in Memory he lives:
 So, in spirit, unto some
 He a subtler soul doth come:
And he never takes, but gives.

While his song the old doth drown,
 Let us neither seek nor grieve:

But that sight and sound believe
Which he cherished as his own;
And if evermore his face
Hid from sight of eyes shall be,
Know that he at last is free,
And has reached a heavenly place.

WHEN THE EVENT IS RIPE.

WHEN the event is ripe,
Matured in patient peace,
Truth, swollen to a flood,
Cuts riverlike her way,
In peace or stained with blood.

O Heart of Youth, grown ripe
Before the people's day!
Wave her white banner high;
Keep back the pain and crime,
And, bloodless, slay the Lie!

THE END OF A TASK WELL DONE.

THE end of a task well done
　　Is the hour of jubilee:
Another must be begun,
　　But the bondage to this is free,
And the sense that the task with the heart is
　　　　one,
　　Is the joy it brings to thee.

So hands and minds and hearts
　　Unite to bring us bliss:
The highest of our arts
　　Is never the hight to miss:
And they who here perform their parts
　　Will learn that heaven is this.

YEARNING.

THE children cry for the ships,
　　But the sails heed not their call;
　　　　They are set to the wind of the sky,
　　　　And never a weakling's cry
　　Can swerve them, one or all,
　　Nor the song of a siren's lips.

O Love on life's ocean plain,
That sailest the way of the sky!
Like a child I yearn and call;
Thou hearest each cry and all,
But makest me no reply;
Yet the loss of thy sail is gain:

For thy flight it stirs me so,
That I cry no more for aught
But the breeze of the wind above,
That unto the heaven doth move
When hearts, like ships, sail out
Where the winds of heaven blow.

VALOR.

BRAVE is that soldier who has faced the foe
In his own breast, and laid his foeman low.

And glory-winner over all is he
Whose magic makes his foes his friends to be.

INSUFFICIENCY.

ART thou that peerless majesty
Whom he should meet who opes to thee
His heart's estate, and says so free:
"Come in, My Friend?"

I, who vowed love, and bore me like a flame
Steadfast as one that out of heaven came,
Found me too poor, too weak to bear that name.

All veiled I stand, shamed by this name of thine,
Who should be open-eyed to be Thy Friend.

Here let me stand, hid from thy noble eyes,
Who, blind, sought love, nor dreamed of majesty;
My part to wait, and lose and fall and rise
Till I can answer back with veilless eyes
And soul that love indeed beyond descries,
Thy greatening call, that bids me mount toward
Love,
To meet the heart of love in thee, My Friend.

AT THE THRESHOLD.

LEAVE thy heart wide open, "Welcome" on the
   door;
 Into thy life let every sweet breath float.
 Now is thy conquest,—not another year,
 Not another day; and here, right here,
 In this short fight wherein shall be thy part,—
 Even where thou art,—is Everlasting Life.

MOONLIGHT IN DECEMBER.

BEFORE the ways get dry of rain,
 Or frost has ceased to wet the ground,
 Sudden the heavens are clear again,
  And in the sky the moon is round.

 Along the hight o'er which she sails
  The way is starred and silver-blue;
 And from the air my heart inhales
  New breath, as though from heaven it drew.

 How keen the change! If, night on night,
  This sudden June might re-appear,
 My spirit should exert its might,
  That droops in duller atmosphere.

A hundred thoughts that choke and die
　　Would rise to stir the hearts of men
If through the air and through the sky
　　June would transform the earth again.

But we must faintly breathe our love,
　　And long for breath to set it free,
Our hearts oppressed by clouds above,
　　And choking airs where'er we be.

Yet, in the memory of sights
　　Like this, sprung sudden on our eyes,
A joy shall last, and in dark nights
　　Shine out to make in hearts new skies.

ONCE.

ONCE is a time that cometh o'er and o'er,
　　And maketh new time fragrant with its
　　　　breath—
A time that lives beyond this air of death,
　　And shall increase its glory more and more
In that new land where true love prospereth.
　　Not half so sweet is all that went before;
And this is all the heart remembereth.

ANOTHER MAID.

WHO loves thee, and loves not
    A maid thou canst not see,
Hid in the heaven of thought,
    Cannot thy true love be.

Oh, yield thyself to none
    That sees not one above
Thyself; that loves alone
    Thyself, and loves not Love.

THE ESSENTIAL.

NOT half the wisdom that my mind can see,
    Not half the beauty that my heart can feel,
Holds any book of all that sacred be,
    Nor half to me can other souls reveal.
I must drink deeper than the sea of speech;
Discard the lore of them that letters teach;
Draw from the springs that fed the conquerors,
And feel in me the life that in God stirs.

EVANESCENCE.

READING Gray's Elegy, to-day, one said:
"Too great is he to lie among the dead;
Yet he who wrote of graves is seen no more,
And none his virtues writeth o'er and o'er."

O who is great, of those alive or dead,
When like a candle's flame our breath is sped?
Who but a day may linger at his ease,
And ponder those who died, and write their elegies?

Yet, over grave and breathing dust, unseen
Stands Life, the Great, immortal and serene;
Life hath not died, though sons of Life be dead;
Life will not die, that hath all living fed,
And yet shall feed beyond the break of death,
And fill anew with his undying breath.

The sense that Christ and Shakespeare still should
    live
Is one with that for all the world who strive
To live unceasing; and the promise made
By Christ to conquer death is in all nature laid.

No graveyard shall endure, or be
To human hopes a ceaseless mockery:
    Dust shall not cover ever

16

The time-infracted frame,
Or stay the strong endeavor
Of men of noble name:
Life shall destroy all deadness,
And set the grave-bound free,
And none shall sing death's sadness,
In days that are to be.

TO BROTHERS FAR AWAY.

BROTHERS far away, whom never I am like to
see again,
I would waft you grateful incense from the garden
of my heart;
Ye have strengthened me in happiness, and merged
away my pain,
And I know no jubilant conquest, but in it ye have
part.

In the clear of early morning ye are with me as of
old,
And at night your presence soothes me like the fragrance of a flower;

Ye may never read my writing, but must feel my
    spirit's fold,
In a hundred happy silences at morn and evening
    hour.

Near or far, we in each other shall take boundless
    hearts'-delight,
And in every word I utter in the measure that is
    dear,
I shall feel the happy urging of your poet-spirits'
    might,
And the far shall not be foreign, and the near shall
    be most near.

COMING LOVERS.

AS many as the roses on the tree
    When last I saw Maruna's fading face
Shall the new lovers of the summer be;
    For Time still runs his Death-unhindered
    race;
And yet, Love outlives Time, as she to me
    Outlives the day when last I saw her face.

O Great-heart Love, our everlasting guest!
  Sun, Moon and Stars may drop from out
      their place;
A myriad lovers yearly sink to rest;
But Memory shall prosper by thy grace,
  And Life shall be renewed with all thy
      zest;
For thou, O Love ! thou makest time and
    place.

THE LAST GIFT.

HERE is a rose for thee,
    Sign of a hopeless quest,
      Token of broken trust:
    Wear it not on thy breast;
      Trample it deep in the dust,
As thou hast trampled me.

Then, in the days to be,
    When roses are white, and rust
      Covers what thou hast confessed,
      And this thou rememberest,
    Think of me if thou must,
But think what thou didst to me.

MATURITY.

WHILE the leaves are waiting, browning on
    the tree,
    Ere the wind shall take them, and scatter
      on the ground,
In my heart I ponder a greater mystery—
    How change, unseen and hurtless, goes on
      and makes no sound:

For when the life-leaf withers and falls like
    these I see,
    No change is there but this unseen that
      makes new life abound:
So that when spring arises, beneath her green
    shall be
    A finer scent and flavor to tell the heart is
      sound.

THE ENEMY.

WHEN Death makes seeming conquest of thy
    friends,
I say to thee, go on thy way unharmed:
No bolt of Death can more than flash on thee
The lightning of its fury; it cannot

Destroy thee, cannot break thy strength, nor e'en
Appall thee as it doth appall the world;
It can but change thy semblance, bate thy breath;
For thou art strong with Life, and Life breaks
        down
The brittle, ghastly battlements of Death.

IN GOD'S SHELTER.

THY shelter in the storm was dear
    When, hurt by stones the careless threw,
I drew away and found Thee near,
    Who knew the bitterness I knew.

More dear each year Thy shelter grows
    As, storm grown hurtless, heart grown strong,
I live in Thy divine repose,
    And by love's conquest conquer wrong.

Up through Life's years to airs sublime
    I mount, and if through sleet or sun,
I love life more, and seek more time,
    Since Thou and I, O God, are one.

TO R. W. G.

TO Richard Watson Gilder,
Of happy rhyme the builder,
On his marriage:
He was wedded once to Verse,
And he never sought divorce;
But he sets his heart to rhyme
With a songless maid's this time,
And I fling my rice of song
In a slipper ten lines long,
To his carriage.

UNUTTERED.

WHAT is so near, yet cannot be read,
As the thought in a maiden's mind?
The key to her lips I could find—
And the words were true that she said;
But the thought that remained behind,
That I knew was true and kind,
That made her as still as the dead,
Only a kiss defined.

DEDICATION OF AN ALBUM.

LARGE Heart, whose name is writ
   In hundred other hearts indelibly,
Here is my name, and o'er and under it
   I write unseen the thought I keep for thee;
Thine to bear on till in old-age you sit,
   And, as I think of you, you think of me.

GOD AND MAN.

BEAUTY revolving all the year;
   The silent might of stream and stone;
Majestic grandeur like a throne
Where mountains unseen summits rear;
An endless train of loving lives;
A boundless scope of varying plan
Are saying: Great are God and man,—
The One who speaks, the one who strives.

For beauty were not, were no eyes
To see; the might of stone and stream
Were vain: there were no mastering dream
If man saw not the mountains rise;

No pulse responsive thrilled to God,
And half at fault were all his plan,
(For half of God indeed is man)
Did man not glorify the sod.

LOVE IN MEMORY.

ALL the way I went that day to the place where
    my Love waited
    Was charmed with strange new music that
        thrilled my fleeting feet ;
The air was thick with beauties, and each
    bloom, each bird was mated—
    I could hear the faintest raptures flooding
        noises of the street.

As a flower doth leave its fragrance in the
    space it once did visit ;
    As a sound of lofty music keeps its soul
        where once 'twas heard—
So she fills that place of meeting with a mem-
    ory exquisite,
    That is sweet of kiss and bosom-swell and
        one low-breathéd word.

24

THE GREETING.

[Read by Robert Adams, at a reception given to Chief Robert A. McWhirr, on his return to Fall River, Mass., from Scotland, by Clan McWhirr, in the Fall of 1890.]

WE have come to welcome you home
　Over the wide sea-foam,
Robert, Chief of the Clan;
And "Welcome!" says every man.

And how has it gone wi' ye
　Over the foaming sea?
We have long waited ye come
Back to your Yankee home,

And wondered, as over the heath
　Ye pattered wi' fainting breath,
And over the lochs sae grand
Ye sailed, in yer ain home land,

If ye might come back at a'
　To bring us yersel' and a'
The beautiful things that your een
In that lan' o' our hearts ha' seen.

We can feel the same joy that ye felt
　As adoun by the hearth ye knelt
Where the auld and the young once were
In the days that can be no more;

We can sing the same song ye sang
In yer thocht as in sport ye sprang
In the games that ye used to play
In the days that are far away.

And now, wi' your heart once more
On the sands of the Yankee shore,
We sing and we gie ye the sign
O' the brothers of Auld Lang Syne.

Joy, Robbie, to be once more
On the dear New England shore,
And to feel the warm blood stir
In the hands of the Clan McWhirr !

We come, young hearts and old,
Young men that their sweethearts fold,
Old men that have not outgrown
The love that their youth has known,—

We come to welcome you home:
With a three-times-three we come,
Robert, the Chief of the Clan;
And "Welcome!" says every man.

RECOGNITION.

THOU canst not go so far but thou wilt find
    Some feature of thyself in human kind;
Nor shut thyself so close but some will see
    Trace of themselves, or glad or sad, in thee.

Since, then, thou art with all mankind at one,
    And all mankind are likewise one with thee,
O Friend! the barrier of thy pride take down,
    And happiness shall come to thee and me.

LOSS.

WHEN I behold a figure, white and strong,
    By Death transfigured from a weak estate,
I grieve not that the slayer did me wrong,
    For he, despite of life, hath made him great
Who passed away; and Life, that doth prolong
    Death's sudden glory, still doth keep my
        mate.

RESOURCE.

ONE is the stream I drink from night and day :
  In weakness and in strength, in joy and pain :
The everlasting ocean of God's Love.

Whence cometh any power of happiness?
Whence, means to rise from yesterday's defeat?

O ever, ever flooded with that tide,
My soul shall rise, my heart rejoice and sing,
And high or low, weak, strong, in bliss or pain,
Loved or unloved, meaneth not anything.

SLEEP.

SLEEP is the guest that all bid come again.
  O soother of my fluttering frame,
    And strengthener of my whole estate,
When I have played Life's little game,
    Still let me on thee wait :
Be with me all my days, and then remain
When Death appears, to ease me of his pain.

THE GIFT.

FOR those who have hope,
　　And those who have none;
Whom the world doth approve,
　　Whom it flingeth a stone;
For weaklings who grope
　　In a dark of their own,
Or for strong and self-centered
　　Who bow but to One;
For the crowd many-minded,
　　Good, guilty and all,
Here's Love—and Love scorns not
　　If men rise or fall.

SIGHT.

TO SEE the glory of the day,
　　E'en when it fades away,
With the same eyes
Wherewith we saw it rise,
Is to behold, from our low hight,
Constant, the greatness of the Infinite.

To keep, in all the dull, dark hours,
The beauty of the flowers,

So that the last dead leaf
Shall give the heart no grief,—
All fadeless, dreamful, dear,—
Is to bear with us everywhere God's beau-
    ty all the year.

A LOVE SONG.

IT WAS once a sweet time, I hear all things say
    As they fade away :—
Birds that wing like fleet time, roses on the
       spray—
Everything I meet, chime in this doleful lay,
    Gliding to decay.

But to me 'tis meet time, then my muse doth
      say ;
Come and go, or stay,
Every breath's a sweet time, every motion gay ;
Of your death in sleet time, or your bright
      array,
    I make roundelay ;

And if others beat time when my rhymes I say,
    I heed not, but they:
For in me is sweet time while the seasons stay,
And I can repeat time when they go away:
    So I sing to-day:

They knew not a sweet time who in sorrow say
    As they fade away,
It was once a sweet time,—else the time would
    stay:
Love doth make a sweet time of a mortal day,
    And it lasts for aye.

RESOLVE.

IF IT should be too late to mend the way
    My feet have made in life's all-conscious clay,
Where every footprint lasts till Judgment Day,
'Tis not too early to make prints anew,
For life flows fresh o'er life, and hides from view,
As waters hide the footmarks on the shore,
The sins that can be blotted nevermore.

New hope each day arises with the sun—
A way outspread o'er which no feet have run—

And night has made me strong, if lost or won
The day gone by; and thrilled with love of all
Dear hearts that sought my heart straight through
    its wall—
Great hearts that like a perfume entered through
The gateway of my life before I knew—
I take new steps, and thrill my followers' feet,
Joy-laden air my feast of heavenly meat,
And sight on every side blooms rare and sweet;
This day, whatever other days have been,—
How sad the weight of ignorance and sin—
God's face shall light the way my feet go in.

VICTORY.

IN THE stillness of my chamber
    I heard the call to arms,
And lone and single-handed
    Went forth to war's alarms.
Now in my silent chamber
    Peace is my royal guest,
And I ask my heart the question,
    Can I meet his lofty test?

Oh, easy were strife in battle,
　And soon a thousand slain;
But who shall wear a garland
　If Selfishness remain?
Peace cannot crown me victor
　For the quenching of Hate's flame
If I march not in the silent ranks
　That bear Love's holy name.

A BEAUTY.

I WONDER if she knows
　How beautiful she is?
No mirror can disclose;
My heart but dimly shows
　The beauty that she is.

But well I know she knows
　How beautiful Love is;
For like a bending rose
Her heart she doth disclose,
　With all Love's sweetnesses.

She knows enough who knows
   How beautiful Love is:
Blind to all other shows
Is she: her beauty grows
   The beauty that Love is.

MUSIC IN THE NIGHT.

A SOUND of music waking one from sleep,
   Oh, how it sets the tender chords a-playing!
And as it dies upon the airy deep,
   It seems as if the heart in dreams were straying.

O ecstasy that I have known long since,
   And long to know again, awake or sleeping,
Thou lingerest without my gate, the prince
   Of mystic charmers in my Father's keeping.

THE WEALTH OF SILENCE.

WHAT holds the silence that I have not heard?
    Withdrawing from the whispers of sweet
        maids,
From sounds of winds among the shining blades,
And sympathetic twitters of a bird;
From strains of happy music from the throats
Of children through the green woods wandering;
From floating far-off melody from boats
Which bear a band of buglers pleasuring;
From cries, as frosty-crystal as the snow,
Of children in their low-set chariots
As, thrilling with the zest cold sports impart,
O'er ice and down long, rough-ribbed hills they go:
Still is the Night, and these sounds come no more:
What if no more I hear them, nor the roar
Of hundred grating noises that I hear,
Lost in the well of silent atmosphere?
Is the deep silence full of happiness?
Death makes no answer, for Death's soul is dumb:
But I can feel in Life, past Death, and far
Beyond the farthest vision of a star,
That silence grows, as sound and noise grow less,
The life of all that is and is to come.

A NIGHT-SONG.

IF I might toss a rose
    Where she is resting,
And break her soft repose,
    My love attesting,

O how this heart would rest,
    And hers go dreaming
There in her sacred nest
    With love's sweets teeming!

If from her slumber she
    But rose and met me,
Set from my longing free,
    I should not fret me.

If I might toss a rose
    Where she is resting,
And break her soft repose,
    My love attesting;—

But, till the night goes past.
    I'll hide my sorrow:
My heart must keep its fast
    For feast to-morrow.

THE MUSIC OF MY LOVE.

WHEN the chimer strikes the bells,
　　All the harmony that stirs
　　To his touch, and soft recurs,
It is drownéd in the swells
　　　Of the music in my heart
　　As I touch my hand to hers,
　　　And the chimes immortal start.

THE LOSS OF A DAY.

BEHOLD the Day new-born,
　　Says Night, that steals away;
　　And hold him while ye may:
A whole world is forlorn
　　For loss of Yesterday.

CAMILLE.

WHAT was her dying strain, O sweet ro-
    mancer?
  Sang she of beauty or a passing fashion?
My heart may well anticipate your answer:
  She breathed the music of eternal passion!

www.ingramcontent.com/pod-product-compliance
Lightning Source LLC
Chambersburg PA
CBHW030914260626
47169CB00008B/2840